Hand of Blood

by

Charles Butler

Illustrated by Dylan Gibson

First published in 2009 in Great Britain by
Barrington Stoke Ltd
18 Walker St, Edinburgh, EH3 7LP

www.barringtonstoke.co.uk

ISBN: 978-1-84299-665-2

Printed in Great Britain by Bell & Bain Ltd

A Note from the Author

Isn't it great how we can make our own bodies do what we ask them to? We put one foot in front of the other, catch a ball, even talk – it's easy to forget just how amazing that all is, because we do it all the time. We only think about it when things begin to go wrong. When we trip up, or stammer, or drop the easy catch – then, suddenly, our bodies seem like strangers to us. Then we can see how fantastic the human body is. But by that time it's too late. We've lost control. The body has ideas of its own ...

For my mother

Contents

Chapter 1
Jet

"Blast! No milk!"

That was my dad, shouting from the kitchen. He was making pancakes, like he did every Sunday. Like most Sundays, he had run out of milk.

"Meg, can you run and get some?" he called.

"OK, Dad," I said from the sofa.

"Take Jenny," he added. "You know she likes to go."

So Jenny and I went to the shop at the end of the street. I'm 17, but Jenny is only 6, and she held my hand tight.

Halfway to the shop was Kidd's Yard. It was just an empty bit of ground, really, with a shed along one side. There was always a radio playing, and a car up on bricks. Some days Mr Kidd was working on the car. You'd see his legs sticking out from under it. Then there were his two dogs. One was OK – a dizzy yellow mutt called Amber. The other was Jet. Jet was a brute. He flung himself against the fence when people walked past, barking like mad. Jet scared me. I was glad there was a bolted gate between Jet and me.

We didn't spot Mr Kidd that day. But he wasn't far away. His tools were by the car, and the radio was loud. Amber and Jet were sniffing around on the far side of the yard. They didn't see us go by.

It was a hot, hot day. Too hot for pancakes. When we got to the shop we bought ice-cream.

"Dad won't mind," I said. But we took our time coming back, just in case.

We were almost past Kidd's Yard again when Jenny tugged at my hand. She said softly, "Meg, look – the gate's not locked."

Most days the gate was shut with a bolt, but today it was hanging open. We hadn't seen that when we passed before.

Maybe the dogs heard us talking. Jet looked up and saw us.

He saw the open gate.

I try not to think about what happened next. Jet raced across the yard, faster than I have ever seen an animal move. He jumped at Jenny, and knocked her over like a skittle.

I heard her scream, and then Jet was on top of her, and the scream stopped.

I just sprang at them. I was yelling, kicking Jet's ribs. Everything was a mess of fur and teeth. Jet made this rasping noise at the back of his throat, not like a dog at all. I pulled at his legs – and then he let go of Jenny and went for me. I grabbed his collar, but he twisted and I felt his teeth bite deep into my hand.

I tried to pull my hand back, but Jet's jaw was strong and his teeth were sharp. I felt them dig in as I tried to get away. I felt them tear into my flesh. Amber was whimpering and barking close by, as if she was scared too.

Mr Kidd came running out of the shed. "Jet! Jet! Back off!" He swore at Jet, but Jet took no notice.

I think I fainted, then. I know I fell, and struck my head on a stone step as I hit the ground. Something went *CRACK*. The last thing I remember was the sticky taste of my own blood.

Chapter 2
In the Clinic

After that there was nothing for a while. White rooms, bright lights, bandages. It was like a dream.

Then, one day, I opened my eyes and saw my father's face. He was smiling at me proudly, like I'd just won a medal. He was smiling – but his eyes were sad.

"Meg, love," he said. That was all he could say.

Suddenly I was wide awake. I knew there was something he did not want to say. Panic flashed through me. "Jenny! Is she OK?"

"Jenny's fine," said Dad. "She only got a few cuts, in the end. Thanks to you." He gave me that funny smile again. "You saved her life."

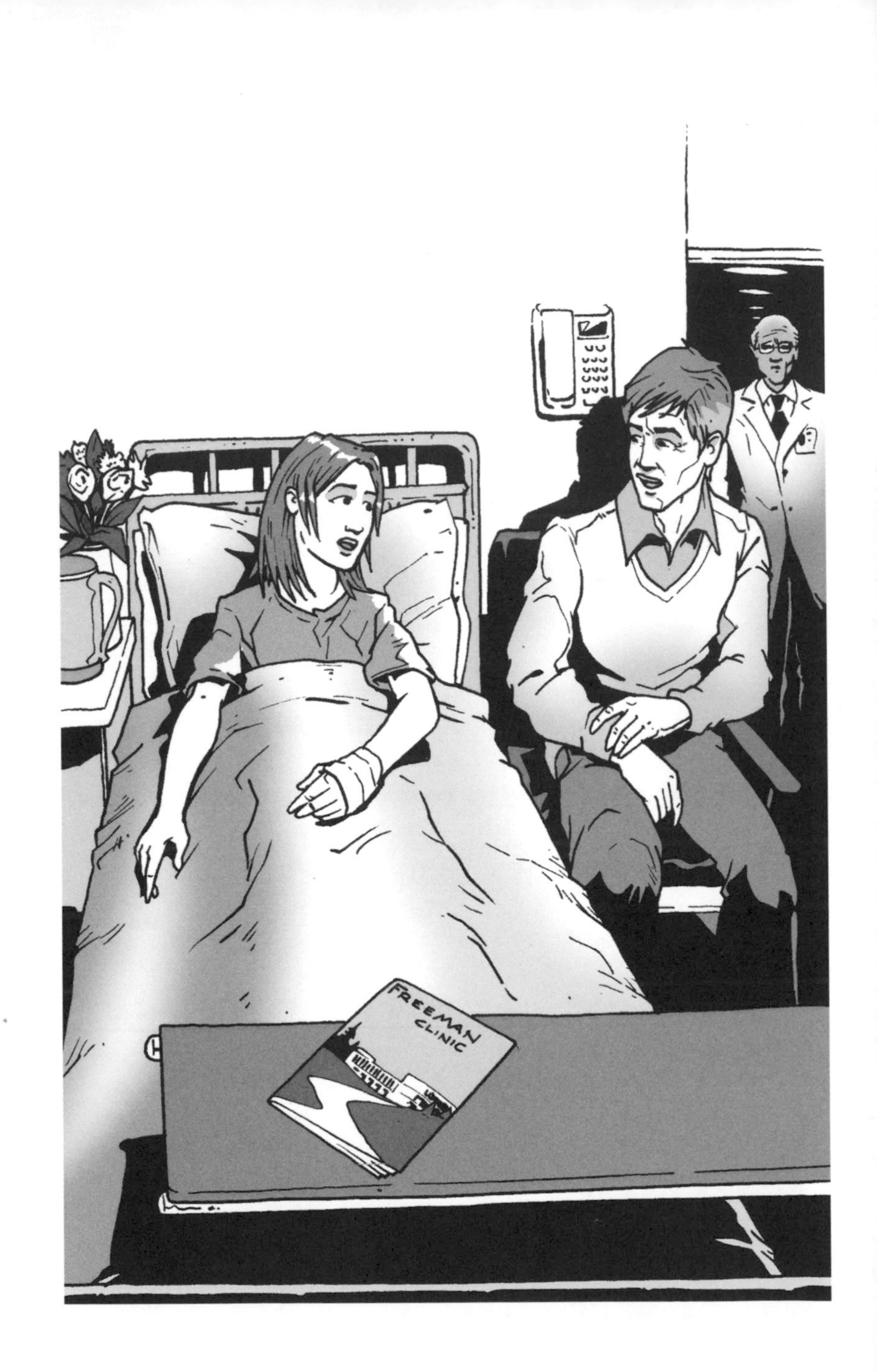
FREEMAN
CLINIC

I took a deep breath. "Thank God."

"You were very brave, taking on that dog. They had to put it down, you know."

I looked around me. I was in a neat, white room, with flowers by the side of my bed. A booklet lay beside it, with the words FREEMAN CLINIC printed in red.

I'd heard of the Freeman Clinic. That smart place on the edge of town.

"It's you we've been worried about," Dad said, with a frown. "How is your head?"

"Hurts a bit," I said with a weak smile. "I've had worse."

"Good, good," he said. Without meaning to he looked quickly down at my hand, lying on the bed.

I gulped, as I remembered. My hand!

I dared to look – and there it was. The hand Jet had bitten to shreds.

But it was perfect. No scars, no stitches. Not a mark on it. Just one bandage, tied around my wrist.

I moved my fingers. They felt a little stiff, and there was a tweak of pain near my wrist, but that was all.

"But I remember ..." I began. "That dog. Jet. He chewed my fingers. I remember."

Dad said, "I won't lie to you, Meg. Your hand was a mess. The doctors tried to save it. But it was too badly hurt."

I didn't understand, at first. "What do you mean?"

I saw now that there was a man standing behind Dad – a young doctor. "Another girl was brought to the Clinic the same day as you," he said. "She was around the same age, same size. She'd had an – an accident, and sadly she died. We needed to decide what to do, fast. We weren't able to ask you, so your father agreed ..."

My dad said very fast, "Meg, that hand used to be hers."

"What? You can't swap people's hands like that!" I cried. "Can you?"

"We've been working on it here at the Clinic," said the doctor. "We've found a way to connect the hand so it will take orders from your brain, just like your old one did. You're one of the first to try it."

I looked down at the hand again. It was very like mine. But now I could see that it wasn't my hand after all. The fingers were a bit too slim, a bit too long. I could see a

mark where one of them had worn a ring, not very long ago.

I told my fingers to waggle. They waggled.

"Wave," I told the hand.

The hand waved back.

"It's amazing," I said. I was stunned, more than anything. Was I still dreaming?

The doctor was looking at me. He wrote things down. "Splendid!" he said, looking pleased. “I’ve never seen one take so fast. I must tell Doctor Freeman. He will want to see you right away.”

The doctor was right. The hand worked perfectly. The fingers did just what they were told. Even the doctors were amazed. No one could hide the place where they had fixed it to my arm, but I wore a wrist band to cover the wound.

But I still did not feel it was part of me. The more I stared at it, the more it looked like the hand of a stranger.

“Who was she?” I asked Dad a few days later. The mark made by the ring was fading, but I could still see it. “Who was the dead girl?”

“Does it matter?” he said.

“She must have been someone! She had a name!”

“She was just a girl,” he said. “A girl who died. She was unlucky. Maybe it’s better not to know.”

But I needed to know. Every time I looked at my hand I wondered.

"Who *are* you?" I asked the hand.

But how can a hand speak?

Chapter 3
Whose Hand?

I saw Doctor Freeman every day. He did tests to find out if my hand was working properly.

"Can you touch the tips of your middle finger and your thumb?" he asked.

I did that.

"Good!" he said, and wrote it in his book. "Now, let's see how much feeling you have in those fingers. Look away, please. What kind of cloth is this?" He ran some cloth over my finger. "Silk or velvet?"

"Velvet."

"Good!" He wrote that in his book too.

He wrote everything in that book.

After a while he got me to hold a pen. It was easy. He made me copy shapes, then draw. He kept telling me how pleased he was with the way things were going. “It’s like that hand *wants* to be part of you,” he said. And we talked, of course. We talked for hours – about Dad and Jenny and movies and school. I liked Doctor Freeman.

One day, after we’d been chatting a while, he stopped suddenly. “Meg, what’s that?” he asked.

“What?”

"There," he said. "On the drawing pad."

I looked. And the pen fell from my hand.

All the time we talked I had still been drawing. I hadn't even known I was doing it. But the picture wasn't my usual style. I'm pretty rubbish, but this was a real artist's work. The picture showed a young woman and a man. They were smiling and standing by a farm gate, and they had their arms round each other. She was looking at me out of the picture. She looked so happy!

“I didn’t do that,” I said.

“You did, you know. I was watching you.”

“I didn’t! That wasn’t me!”

“I see,” he said, with a frown.

And he wrote it in his little book.

****

It wasn’t *me* that had done that drawing: it was the hand. The other girl’s hand. I knew then that I *had* to find out about her.

No one would tell me anything, but this is not a big town. If a girl had died here, it would be in the newspaper. I went to the TV room and looked at the old papers there. Yes! There was the one from the day after I was attacked. On page three I found what I was looking for.

STUDENT KILLED IN HIT AND RUN

Becky Green, a student at Dale School of Art, died in hospital yesterday after being run down at a crossing near her home. A brilliant artist, Becky was about to take up a job at one of the big London fashion houses. Police are asking anyone who saw what happened to contact them.

Next to the story was a photo of a smiling girl with long, blonde hair.

I knew her at once. She was the girl I had drawn in my picture.

"Meg? What are you doing?" asked one of the nurses.

FILM
NEWS
STUDENT KILLED IN HIT AND RUN
LOCAL
CONTINUED...
LOW COST LOANS
29·7 APR
FREEMAN CLINIC

“What?” I said, looking round in surprise. “Oh, I’m sorry.”

I had not meant to, but I had torn the page out of the paper and crumpled it into a ball. The fingers of my hand were white, they were pressing it so hard.

Chapter 4
Home

Weeks went by. I was back home, and life was normal again. *Almost* normal. I couldn't help looking at my new hand all the time. I tried to tell myself it was a part of me now. It did everything I wanted it to, didn't it? It brushed my teeth, scratched my head and lifted food to my mouth. But still ...

It sounds stupid, but I just didn't *trust* it. Not after that drawing.

I had bad dreams, too. In one, I was back in Kidd's Yard. I was looking down at my left hand and seeing nothing but a ragged stump. Jet and Amber were in my dream, and Mr Kidd was throwing them something to eat. "There, Jet! There, Amber!" he was crying. "Eat up! Good dogs!"

I knew what they were eating. I could feel their wet tongues lick the tip of each finger.

I sat up, wide awake. What a nightmare! My hand still felt wet from the dogs' tongues. Wet and sticky ...

I turned on the light by my bed. I was right. My hand *was* still wet.

It was wet with blood.

I screamed then, but stopped myself before I woke anyone up. At last I saw that I wasn't bleeding. The blood must have come from somewhere else. I ran to the bathroom

and turned on the tap. I scrubbed and scrubbed until my hand was clean.

Where had the blood come from? I wished I knew.

I stumbled back to my room and got into bed. Then I saw it, on the floor. It was the meat knife from our kitchen – and there was blood on it.

What had I done?

I kicked the knife under the bed, and lay awake till morning, too scared to think.

****

The next day the door bell rang early. There was shouting, too. "Open up! I know she lives here! Open up!"

My dad went down to open the door, still yawning.

It was Mr Kidd – and his face was dark with anger. He looked right past my dad, and saw me on the stairs behind.

"You!" he yelled, pointing at me. "You did it! You killed my dog! You killed Amber!"

"Stop shouting at my family and tell me what you want," said Dad coldly.

"I saw you last night," Mr Kidd went on, still looking at me. "Hanging about in the yard. It was dark, but I'd know you anywhere. And this morning, Amber's dead. Stabbed! Wasn't it enough that Jet had to be put down? Did you have to kill my Amber too? Don't tell me you didn't do it!"

76

"Of course she didn't do it," said Dad. "She was at home all night. We all were. You're raving. Now, get off this step before I call the police."

He shut the door in Mr Kidd's face.

"He's mad," he muttered. "As if you'd do a thing like that."

I ran to my room, and pulled the bloody knife from under the bed. There was a sheet of paper on the floor beside it, that I hadn't

I Did it for you. Now do it for Me

seen last night. Some words were written there in brown, dry blood:

"I DID IT FOR YOU. NOW DO IT FOR ME."

Chapter 5
Pay Back

I had to find out about Becky. I went to the crossing where she was killed. I hung around outside her Art School, and tried to bump into her mates. They looked at me like I was sick. “Leave her alone,” they said. “She’s *dead!*”

"Why are you doing this?" I asked the hand. "What do you want?"

I must have *looked* sick, too, talking like that in the street. Talking to myself.

I hung out there for three days, rain and shine. I sat in the cafe across from the Art School, watching the gates. I knew I was waiting for something – for *someone* – but I didn't know who.

On the fourth afternoon I saw him. A tall guy, dressed like a student. I didn't know him at first, then I saw it was the young man from the picture that my hand had drawn. The one by the farm gate.

I felt my fist go tight. My hand – Becky's hand – was squeezing every drop of anger out of itself. And, as the hand squeezed, the anger poured into *me*. Anger flooded my mind.

Not just anger. I started to remember things.

I ran across the street. “You! Kevin Taylor!”

The man stopped. He turned, slowly. I saw him trying to work out who I was. “Do I know you?” he asked.

“You should know me! You bought the ring that used to go on this finger.” I pointed at him.

“I don’t know what you mean,” he said.

He tried to sound bored, but I could see fear in his eyes.

"Liar! You were going to marry Becky Green, weren't you? Until she called it off."

"What are you talking about?"

"She wanted to go to London – but you weren't having that, were you? You hated that she had more talent than you. You were jealous! You—"

He slapped me hard across the face. Other people had stopped to watch.

Even then, I could not stop Becky's words coming out of my mouth. "That's what you did to her, too, wasn't it?" I sneered. "To keep her in line? And when that didn't work, you stopped her another way. You ran her down!"

"Shut *up*," he said, cold as steel. "Shut up now, you mad bitch, or you'll regret it."

"It's all right," I said. "I've done with talking."

The knife was ready in my hand.

I don't think he saw the blade coming. He didn't move at all – just stood there as it slashed his throat. Blood sprayed, and I heard him choke a bit before he fell at my feet. Then there were people grabbing me, pinning my arms. I heard someone say, "It's Kevin – that crazy girl just went for him." Someone else was screaming, "Get a doctor! And the police!"

The guy who had hold of my arms was saying, “Drop it. Just drop the knife right now, OK? No one else needs to get hurt.”

It didn’t feel real. I was watching myself from the outside, like I was a stranger. I felt my fingers open and the knife dropped to the ground.

“It’s fine,” I said, as they pulled me away. My hand hung limply by my side. “It’s fine. It wasn’t me, you see. It was Becky – and she got what she wanted. She’s gone now. She’s left me.”

"You're not making sense," said the guy who had hold of me. Everyone was standing round.

"But you've got to understand. It was Becky – it was Becky Green's hand. Look!"

They looked.

And I looked.

I looked where my strong new hand had been, a moment before.

The *thing* at the end of my arm was swollen with decay, and half its nails were gone. It had been alive, once.

But now Becky Green's hand was nothing but black and rotting flesh.

Barrington Stoke would like to thank all its readers for commenting on the manuscript before publication and in particular:

Jack Braithwaite
Dan Breckon
Judy Carter-Brown
Peter Dunford
Dawn Groan
Jessica Harrison
Stephen Hill
Scott Howard
Thomas Hutchinson
Nathan Pearson
Leslie Robson

Become a Consultant!

Would you like to give us feedback on our titles before they are published? Contact us at the email address below – we'd love to hear from you!

info@barringtonstoke.co.uk
www.barringtonstoke.co.uk